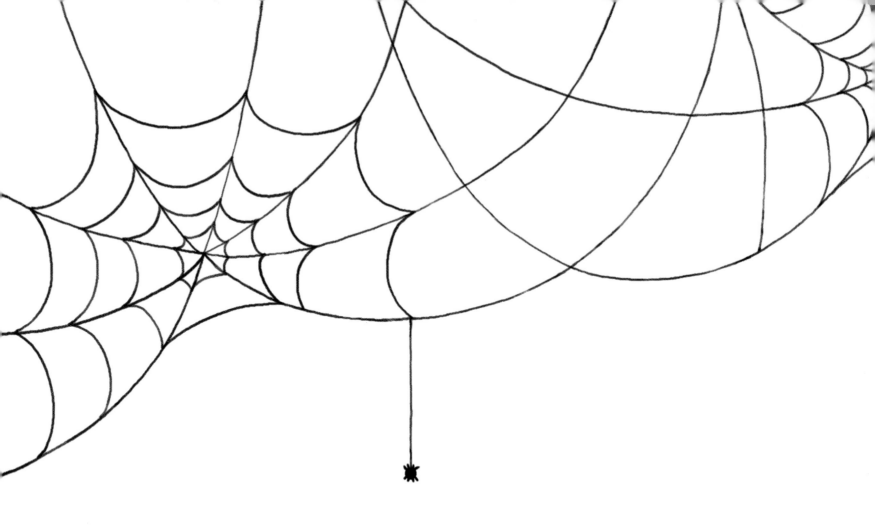

Originally published as *Luuk en Lotje: Het is Halloween!* in Belgium and Holland by Clavis Uitgeverij, Hasselt—Amsterdam, 2017
English translation from the Dutch by Clavis Publishing Inc., New York

Visit us on the Web at www.clavisbooks.com.

Luke and Lottie: It's Halloween! written and illustrated by Ruth Wielockx

ISBN 978-1-60537-411-6

This book was printed in June 2018 at Publikum d.o.o., Slavka Rodica 6, Belgrade, Serbia.

First Edition
10 9 8 7 6 5 4 3 2 1

Luke and Lottie

It's Halloween!

Clavis
NEW YORK

Ruth Wielockx

It's Halloween!
Tonight Luke and Lottie are going trick-or-treating.
"I will be a witch," Lottie announces.
She's already wearing her witch hat.
"And I'm dressing up as a ghost," says Luke.
"I'm going to scare you. Boo-oo!"

"Ahhh!" Lottie screams.
"Look! There's a big spider."
Luke sees it too.
"Mom, help!" he calls.

"That's not a real spider," Mom laughs.
"It's a decoration."
Luke and Lottie carefully touch the spider.
"It's so soft," says Luke.
"But also scary," Lottie thinks.

"I'm making Halloween treats," says Mom.
"Do you want to help?"
Yum! Luke and Lottie want to help!
Luke puts raisin eyes on the banana ghosts.
Lottie makes little pumpkins out of clementines.

"Who wants to make jack-o'-lanterns?" asks Dad.
Dad cuts the top off the pumpkins.
Lottie scoops out the pumpkin seeds with a spoon.

Dad helps the twins make scary faces.
Luke wants one with triangle eyes.
"I want circle eyes on mine," says Lottie.
Mom puts candles in the pumpkins.
"Ooh!" Luke and Lottie look at the dancing lights.

"Time to put our costumes on!" Luke and Lottie cheer.
Dad dresses up too. He is a vampire.
"Help," Dad calls, "I'm being chased by a witch and a ghost!"

The witch, the ghost, and the vampire go trick-or-treating together.
Mom stays at home to hand out sweets.
"Have fun!" she says, waving.

The street is filled with other trick-or-treaters.
There are mummies, zombies, werewolves, skeletons,
trolls, ghosts, and witches.
"Look!" says Dad. "Aunt Tina and Marie are here too."

Aunt Tina is dressed as a mummy,
and Marie is dressed as a witch, just like Lottie.
"Come on," Luke calls impatiently. "Let's get started!"

What's this?
Is it a real witch?
"Hocus pocus. Howl and boo.
I have special treats for you!"
No, it is just a neighbor welcoming
the trick-or-treaters.

Luke, Lottie, and Marie go from house to house.
They ring the doorbell.
"Trick or treat!" they call when the door opens.
Then they get something sweet.

Time to go home.
Luke and Lottie tell Mom all about trick-or-treating.

"Trick-or-treating was fun," says Luke.
"But I'm happy to be home," adds Lottie.
Happy Halloween!